MIKE YOUNG

AND
THE TIME MACHINE
HIJACKED IN SPACE
THE SPACE CIRCUS
THE GHOST ROCKET
THE STOLEN ROCKET SHIP

Illustrations by Rob Lee, David Blake,
and Tony Hutchings

CARNIVAL

Carnival
An imprint of the Children's Division,
part of the Collins Publishing Group,
8 Grafton Street, London W1X 3LA

Published by Carnival 1988

Cartoon films as seen on BBC and
S4C Television, produced by Siriol
Animation for S4C, the Welsh Fourth Channel

Printed and bound in Great Britain by
William Collins Sons & Co. Ltd, Glasgow

ISBN 0 00 194406 1

AND THE TIME MACHINE

Clank! Clank! Boing! Clank!

SuperTed's friend, Spottyman, was building a time machine.

Zonk! Bang! Cling! Bonk!

"Do you have to make so much noise, Spotty?" said SuperTed, walking into Spotty's space lab. "I can hear you at the other end of the space station."

"I've almost finished," answered Spotty. He hammered the last rivet into the side of the machine and stood back. "There! A perfect example of Spotty engineering."

SuperTed looked at Spotty's invention and sighed. It was yellow with green spots. "I don't like the colour scheme, Spotty."

"Hmph!" snorted Spotty. "All the best things have spots. When I travel into the future, I'll probably find that the whole universe is spotty!"

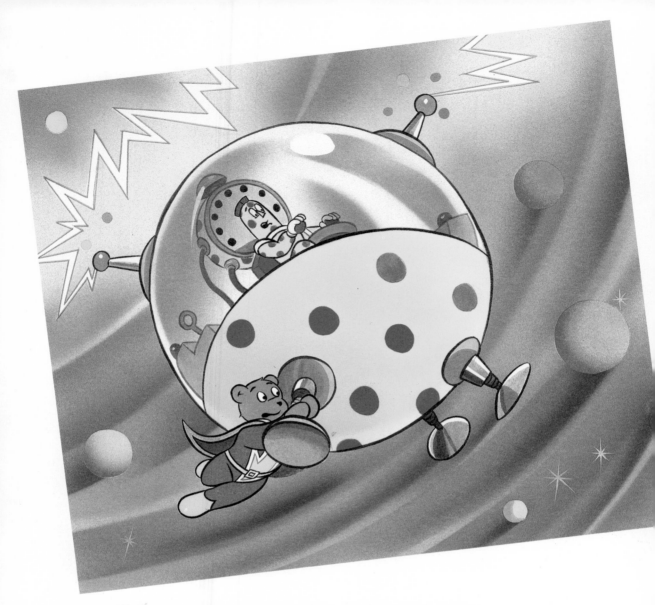

Spotty climbed into his machine and set the controls.

"I think I should come with you," said SuperTed. "You might need my help."

"Nonsense!" Spotty replied. "I'll be fine. In the future, Spotty people will be welcomed everywhere, but teddy bears probably won't exist." Then SuperTed stood back, and Spotty pressed a button on the control panel.

"Goodbye!" yelled Spotty. The time machine began to shake. It bounced and shuddered until the whole space station began to shake with it.

SuperTed muttered his magic word and changed into his special form. Then he grabbed the side of the machine. He was afraid it might fall apart. But as he held on, he began to slip into the future with Spotty and his invention.

It seemed as if the whole universe was spinning around them. Planets and stars whirled past as the machine began to buck up and down like a wild horse.

SuperTed felt sick. All this reminded him of the Big Dipper at the funfair. It churned up his stuffing and made his ears pop. But he held on tight. He knew that if he let go, he would be lost in the future forever.

Gradually, everything slowed down. The spinning stopped, and a green landscape, covered with golden stars, appeared around them. They had landed on a distant planet sometime in the future.

SuperTed and Spotty stood in front of the time machine and gazed at the countryside.

"I can see lots of stars," said SuperTed, "but no spots."

"We've hardly seen anything yet," Spotty replied. "The people that live on this planet are probably even spottier than I am."

At that moment, they heard a shout from behind them. They looked over their shoulders to see a band of small furry creatures hopping down the hill.

None of them had spots. They were all covered in brightly coloured stars.

The creatures crowded around SuperTed and giggled. They were very curious. Some of them sniffed at his fur, and touched him gently on the arm. Others came straight up to him and peered into his eyes. None of them went anywhere near Spotty.

"They obviously think I'm a superior being," said Spotty.

"It's not that," said SuperTed. "I think it's your spots. They're worried they might be catching."

Then the creatures hoisted SuperTed onto their shoulders and carried him towards their village.

"Come on, Spotty!" called SuperTed. "Follow us!"

Spotty was being unfriendly. "You go on," he called back, "I'm going to explore." And with that, he set off in the opposite direction.

When SuperTed saw the village, he had the feeling that he had been there before. There was something familiar about the starry domes, and the creatures hopped around on two legs almost like the hopperoos on Spotty's planet.

The creatures were certainly very friendly. They sang and danced for SuperTed, and gave him strange, starry fruit to eat. SuperTed clapped along with their music and enjoyed himself tremendously.

When the sun dipped under the horizon, he began to worry about Spotty.

"I'll go and find him," he murmured to himself, "before he gets into trouble."

SuperTed walked out of the village and across the starry countryside. "I'm sure I've been here before," he thought.

Soon he came to the time machine. Two of the starry animals were guarding it, but there was no sign of Spotty.

"Have you seen my spotty friend?" SuperTed asked.

The creatures looked at SuperTed in surprise. "He's your friend? Oh dear. They're keeping him shut in a big cave so nobody will catch his spotty disease."

SuperTed looked up at the hillside. At the bottom of a small cliff he could see the dark opening of a cave. It was time to say his magic word, again.

In a flash, he changed into his magic shape, and soared towards the cliff.

When he arrived, he found some of the furry creatures rolling a huge boulder across the mouth of the cave. He fired his rocket boots at full power and headed straight towards them. The creatures turned and ran.

There was a loud crack as SuperTed hit the rock. Large splinters of stone flew into the air and showered down the hillside.

SuperTed strode into the cave. "Spotty! Spotty!" he called. "Are you there?"

There was no reply. Cautiously, SuperTed stepped deeper into the cave. It was dark, and he was frightened.

He edged along a narrow tunnel, calling Spotty's name. Suddenly, he saw a glimmer of light ahead, and he flew towards it. The tunnel opened into a large, underground cavern.

SuperTed saw Spotty at once. Spotty was holding a torch in his hand and examining the cavern wall.

"Look what I've found," he said to SuperTed. "I knew there would be some sign of spotty life."

Sure enough, five green spots were painted on the wall in front of them. The paint was very faded. Now they both knew where they were. This was the Planet Spot, sometime in the distant future.

SuperTed helped Spotty out of the cave.

Later, he explained to his starry creatures that Spotty did not have a disease. His spots were part of his natural colouring. A long time ago, they probably had spots, too, but, over the years, their spots had changed into stars. So there was nothing to be afraid of. It was not very kind to shut someone in a cave because they looked different.

"It's your fault as well," SuperTed said to Spotty. "If you hadn't been so unfriendly, these starry hopperoos would have accepted you for what you are."

Then SuperTed and Spotty climbed into the time machine and said goodbye. Once again the machine shuddered into life, and soon the two friends were spinning backwards in time.

When they got back to the space station, Spotty decided to take the time machine to pieces.

"I'm quite content to live in the present," he said. "There aren't enough spots in the future."

MIKE YOUNG

SUPERTED

IN HIJACKED IN SPACE

Illustrations by Rob Lee
and David Blake

A small spaceship rocketed past the stars. It was yellow with green spots.

Inside were Mr and Mrs Spot, who were on their way to visit their son, Spottyman, and his friend, SuperTed.

"Left hand down a bit," called Mr Spot.

"All right, all right," replied Mrs Spot, who was driving. "I know the way to SuperTed's space station. We've been there hundreds of times."

They were so busy talking, that they did not notice a dark figure drop through the hatch behind them. Before they knew it, a coil of rope dropped over their heads and pinned them to their seats.

"Hi there, you spotty varmints" snarled a deep voice. "This is a hijack."

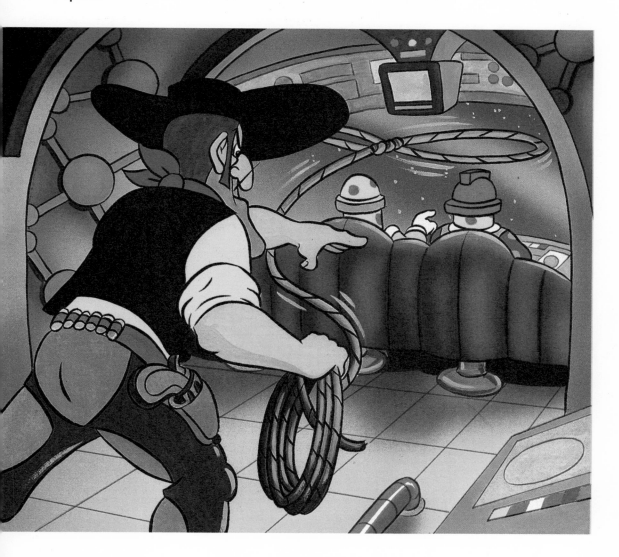

In their space station, SuperTed and Spotty were preparing for
the visit. SuperTed was making the beds in the spare room, and
Spotty was cleaning the carpets with a turbo-vacuum cleaner.

Spotty hummed to himself as he swept the cleaner backwards
and forwards along the tubular corridor, but as he turned
around a trap door opened above him and an ugly face
poked through. Spotty recognised it immediately. It was the evil
Texas Pete!

"Keep quiet or I'll knock your spots off!" hissed Tex as he dropped to the ground.

"I'm not f..f..frightened of you, you silly cowboy," burbled Spotty.

Texas Pete just laughed. "I've got your parents, pimple-head. Now do as I tell you, or you'll never see them again." He pulled a photograph out of his pocket and thrust it in front of Spotty's nose.

Spotty looked at it in horror. It showed Mr and Mrs Spot, tied to the seats of their spaceship. Behind them, Bulk, Skeleton and Tex stood, grinning at the camera.

"Here, measle face, take this" grunted Tex, and he pushed a jar of tablets into Spotty's hand. "Cactus Drops. Put one of these in SuperTed's drink. It'll knock him out for good."

"I can't do that" said Spotty. "SuperTed's my friend."

Tex laughed again. "And remember, if there's any trouble, you'll never see your parents again." With that, he climbed back out of the hatch.

Spotty was worried. SuperTed was his best friend, and he did not want to do anything to harm him, but he also loved his parents very much. He did not want to harm them either.

"What shall I do?" thought Spotty, clutching the jar of Cactus Drops in his hand.

"What's the matter, Spotty?" asked SuperTed, as he finished making a bed.

Spotty looked up, blankly. "Ur....ur..."

"Come on," said SuperTed. "Let's have an astrojuice before your parents arrive."

Spotty followed SuperTed into the space station's kitchen.

"Er..I'll pour it," muttered Spotty nervously, and he pushed past SuperTed and opened the refrigerator. His hands were shaking as he poured out two glasses of the delicious, blue juice.

Then, when SuperTed's back was turned, he unscrewed the jar and dropped one of the tablets into a glass. The drink fizzed for a moment and then was still. Spotty handed the glass to his friend. SuperTed drank it down in one gulp. "Ah... that's better," he said. "Housework makes you so thirsty."

"Did it taste all right?" asked Spotty.

"Don't be silly, Spotty," replied SuperTed. "Astrojuice always tastes delicious."

Before Spotty had time to say anything else, SuperTed's eyes glazed over, and he fell backwards onto the floor with a thud.

Spotty leant over his friend and sobbed, "By the Great Moons of Spot, what have I done?"

As he crouched there, trying to revive his friend, the kitchen door slid open, and in walked Texas Pete, followed by his two cronies, Bulk and Skeleton.

"Bulk! Skeleton!" roared Tex. "Pick up that mangy ball of stuffing and sling him in the hold of our ship. We'll dump him in the galactic wastelands. It'll be centuries before anyone finds him there."

"What about my parents?" asked Spotty.

"Your parents! Ha ha." sniggered Tex. "We'll dump them in the galactic wastelands as well!"

Spotty was hopping mad. He had been cheated. He lunged at Tex and butted him in the stomach. But the tall cowboy stood firm. He picked Spotty up and turned him upside down. Spotty kicked his legs in the air in frustration.

"Put me down, you spotless freak!" he yelled.

But Tex did not put him down. He carried Spotty to the landing platform where his rocket was waiting.

"Head for the far end of the universe, Skeleton!" he shouted, as he stepped into his spaceship. Then he opened the door of the hold, and threw Spotty inside.

"Hello, son," said two voices out of the darkness.

Spotty peered across the dingy hold. There were his parents, standing near the lifeless SuperTed.

"Mum! Dad! Are you all right?"

"Yes," replied Mr and Mrs Spot. "But what's happened to SuperTed?"

"Tex forced me to put Cactus Drops in his drink. He said I'd never see you again if I didn't." Spotty shook his head in despair. "I should have known not to trust him."

"It looks like we've had it, then," moaned Mrs Spot.

"No we haven't," replied Spotty. "SuperTed will save us." Mr and Mrs Spot looked at their son in surprise.

"You see..." continued Spotty. "I have some Cosmic Dust with me."

Spotty pulled a small flask out of his pocket and sprinkled some Cosmic Dust over his friend. Within seconds SuperTed was sitting up and rubbing his eyes.

"Bubbling...Raspberries," he groaned, "what's going on?"

"We're in Tex's rocket," answered Spotty. "We have to get out of here before Tex dumps us in the galactic wasteland."

SuperTed said his magic word. In a flash, he turned into his special form.

"Stand back," he told his friends, before he directed the full force of his rocket boots at the door of the hold. There was a hissing of scorched metal, and the door swung open.

SuperTed surprised Tex and his friends as he charged into the control room. Bulk and Skeleton tried to run for the escape hatch, but they found Spotty and his parents blocking their path.

Tex stood his ground, and when the heroic teddy bear flew towards him, he ducked and sent SuperTed hurtling against the wall.

"You'll pay for that, Texas Pete!" gasped SuperTed, breathlessly. He turned and grabbed Tex's arm. Then he swung the struggling cowboy around in a circle, twirling him over his head.

"Stop! Put me down," moaned Tex in terror. "I give in, put me down!" But SuperTed did not put him down. He bowled Tex along the floor like a ball. Tex slid along the corridor, arriving in the hold with a bump.

Spotty bundled Bulk and Skeleton after him, and soon all three villains were safely locked up.

Later, SuperTed, Spotty and his parents celebrated in the space station.

"Of course," explained Spotty, "I knew I could bring you round with my Cosmic Dust any time I wanted. Otherwise, I would never have put anything in your drink."

"I believe you," said SuperTed, "but next time I have some astrojuice, I think I'll pour it myself."

SUPERTED
AND THE SPACE CIRCUS

SuperTed paced up and down the corridors of his space station. He was very worried. His best friend, Spottyman, had gone to the Playtime Planets for a holiday, and had not come back.

"Bubbling Blancmange! Where is he?" groaned SuperTed. "He should have been back ages ago. He hasn't even sent a message on the videophone!"

There was only one thing for it. SuperTed said his magic word, and then, his red cape flapping behind him, he flew towards the exit hatch.

"Hang on, Spotty, wherever you are!"

With his rocket boots firing at full power, SuperTed shot across space like a bullet. He raced past the Great Bear, and headed towards Orion's Belt. There was no sign of Spotty!

There was quite a commotion around the Playtime Planets. When he arrived, he saw rockets everywhere — short rockets, long rockets, even one rocket with a sidecar. They were all heading in the same direction.

"Where are you all going?" shouted SuperTed.

A strange creature with a long nose poked his head out of a rocket and shouted back. "We're going to the Circus Planet. They've got a sensational new act. They're going to fire a strange Spottyman out of a supersonic cannon!"

SuperTed turned and headed straight for the Circus Planet. There was no time to lose.

The circus was taking place inside a large crater. When
SuperTed landed, he joined a queue of strange space
creatures. Then he sat down on the rim of the crater and
watched the show.

The ringmaster looked very familiar. He had a red coat and
brown riding boots, but, instead of a top hat, he wore a large
cowboy's stetson.

"Orbiting Oranges!" gasped SuperTed. "It's Texas Pete!"

Texas Pete stood in the centre of the crater and cracked a whip. "First, for all you creepy creatures," he snarled, "Tex's Sensational Circus presents...The Impossible Prickle People!"

A troupe of green cactus people rushed on, somersaulted over each other, and formed a pyramid. SuperTed thought they looked very unhappy.

"Next!" yelled Tex, "Tentacles on the Tightrope!"

A creature with even more tentacles than an octopus climbed sadly onto a high tightrope, and started to edge gingerly along it. It swung in the air, a long way from the ground.

"Rocketing Raspberries!" screamed SuperTed, as the creature slipped and fell. But before he could rush to its help, the creature reached up with one of its long, rubbery arms and pulled itself back onto the tightrope.

The crowd sighed with relief.

Tex strode across the ring and grinned wickedly. "And next, ladies and cowpokes!" he sneered. "The Prodigious Parachute Person!"

SuperTed watched in horror as a small creature from the Crazy Planet wearily climbed up a huge ladder. When it got to the top, it dived into the air and plummeted towards the ground. Then, at the last moment, the creature spread its arms, and a parachute opened up from between its shoulders. It landed gently on the ground and gave a sad bow.

"And now," screamed Tex, "the moment you've been waiting for! The Supersonic Spotty Cannonball!"

When he heard this, SuperTed leapt to his feet. "It *is* Spotty! But what is he doing?"

SuperTed watched in horror as Bulk and Skeleton, Tex's two assistants, led the reluctant Spotty to a huge cannon and loaded him into the barrel.

"We will now fire this pimple-headed person into the most poisonous parts of space!" cackled Tex. "He will travel faster than a speeding bullet, and will never return to plague us fun-loving cowboys again!".

There was a crackle as Bulk lit the fuse, and then SuperTed heard the dull thud of an explosion. Spotty exploded from the cannon and shot into the sky.

In a flash, SuperTed was after him. He managed to grab Spotty's foot as he hurtled past, and used his rocket boots to slow him down. Then SuperTed carried his friend to the ground.

"Th..th..thank you, SuperTed," burbled Spotty. "Texas Pete
kidnapped me and forced me to work in his circus.
He's captured creatures from all over the galaxy. None of
them want to be here. If we don't set them free, they'll never
see their homes again."

"Come on, then," said SuperTed. "It's time we taught Texas Pete
a lesson."

Spotty had no rocket pack, and so SuperTed carried him back
towards the crater. When they got there, Texas Pete had
already shut the circus creatures in their cages. Tex hitched the
cages to the back of his rocket, and took off into space.

SuperTed left Spotty on the ground and flew after his old enemy. Tex's rocket shot across the sky, but it was not fast enough to escape SuperTed.

The heroic teddy bear grasped the side of one of the cages, and pulled open the door. The circus creatures were delighted to see him.

"Come on!" said SuperTed. "If we're going to stop Tex, I'll need your help."

Tex had seen SuperTed. He chuckled to himself, and pulled a lever on the control panel. Suddenly the cages came away from the rocket, and dropped towards the ground.

"He...l..p!" screamed the space creatures.

SuperTed turned to the space creature that had walked the tightrope.

"Quick! Grab the rocket with one of your tentacles!" he shouted.

In a flash, the creature stretched out a rubbery arm and caught hold of the back of Tex's rocket.

Tex laughed, and put his rocket into a spin. The creature's arm twisted like a piece of elastic.

"Ouch!" it cried, and let go. Once more, the cages began to plummet towards the ground.

SuperTed flew at Tex's rocket and tore open the hatch. Within seconds he had overpowered Tex and grabbed the controls. He turned the rocket back towards the surface of the planet.

"I just hope I can get to those cages in time!" he gasped.

He need not have worried. As the cages hurtled towards the ground, a blue parachute opened above them. The circus creatures landed safely.

The Prodigious Parachute Person stepped away from the cages and gave a little bow. He had saved his friends.

Later, SuperTed, Spotty and the circus creatures celebrated their freedom with a very special performance. SuperTed did a juggling act, and all the circus entertainers showed off their most spectacular tricks.

As a finale, they loaded Texas Pete into the cannon, and fired him into the loneliest part of space. Everybody cheered. It would be a long time before Tex did any more harm.

MIKE YOUNG

SUPERTED
AND THE GHOST ROCKET

A small, spotty spaceship rocketed through the outer reaches of a distant galaxy. Inside were SuperTed and Spottyman, on their way to the Planet Spot.

Suddenly, SuperTed turned to his friend. "I think I can see something up ahead," he said.

"Don't be silly, SuperTed," answered Spotty. "There's nothing in this part of space. We're millions of miles from the nearest star."

Spotty looked at the radar screen. It was totally blank. There was nothing out there. Or was there?

At that moment, SuperTed and Spotty gasped with horror. Through the cockpit window they could see a huge spaceship, heading straight towards them. They covered their eyes. There was going to be a terrible crash!

SuperTed raced for the controls, but it was too late. There was nothing he could do. The spotty rocket began to turn, but not fast enough to avoid the oncoming spaceship.

Then something very peculiar happened. There was a loud crackle of electricity, and the spotty rocket went straight through the strange spaceship, and out the other side.

"Bubbling Blancmange!" gasped SuperTed.

"B..By the Great Moons of Spot!" burbled Spotty.

They ran to the window and looked behind them. There was a spaceship, glowing with a strange light. They could almost see through it.
"If it didn't show up on the radar..." said Spotty.

"And we passed right through it," continued SuperTed. "Then it must be a ghost rocket!"

"I don't believe in ghosts," said SuperTed.

"Neither do I," said Spotty, "but what else could it be?"

"I don't know," whispered SuperTed, "but whatever it is, I don't like the look of it. Come on, Spotty. Let's get out of here."

Spotty set the controls and the engines began to fire. Soon the two friends were speeding across space. They travelled quite a distance before Spotty dared to look behind them out of the window.

"SuperTed!" groaned Spotty. "That ghost rocket. It's following us."

When SuperTed saw the strange rocket behind them, he
began to panic. "Don't worry, Spotty," he said. "We'll soon lose
that rocket."

He put the spotty rocket into full thrust. The boosters glowed
white hot, and there was a surge of speed as they shot
forward. But the ghost rocket kept up with them.

Then SuperTed began to swing the controls from side to side.
The spotty rocket zigzagged on a crazy course, but the ghost
rocket seemed to match every turn it made.

Suddenly, SuperTed saw a large asteroid ahead of them. "Let's
hide there."

Before the ghost rocket had time to react, SuperTed put the spotty spaceship into a tight spin, dashed behind the asteroid, and landed in a large crater.

"It'll never find us here," he whispered to Spotty. "You wait and see. In a minute, it'll sail right past."

The two friends waited, but the ghost rocket did not sail past. Instead, it arrived in the crater. But it did not arrive out of the sky. It came from underneath the ground.

It had travelled right through the asteroid.

"There's only one thing for it," said SuperTed. "We'll have to go and investigate."

He said his magic word, and changed into his special shape. Spotty pulled on his rocket pack, and soon the two of them were floating across the crater towards the strange spaceship.

"I can't see any hatches," yelled Spotty. "How do we get inside?"

"That's easy," called SuperTed. "This is a ghost rocket. We just walk through the wall."

Then SuperTed stepped forward, and disappeared through the side of the rocket.

Spotty soon followed him. The inside of the rocket looked cold and empty and the walls glowed. SuperTed and Spotty found it difficult to explore. When they tried to walk along a corridor, they would sink through the floor, or stumble through a wall, and find themselves in a different part of the rocket. There was nothing solid in the whole spaceship.

At last they reached the control room. A large pillar of flashing lights and buttons stood in the centre of the room. When Spotty leant forward to press a button, his hand went straight through the pillar.

"By the Bald Birds of Spot!" yelled Spotty. "How do they drive this rocket?"

"Quite easily," replied a soft voice from behind him.

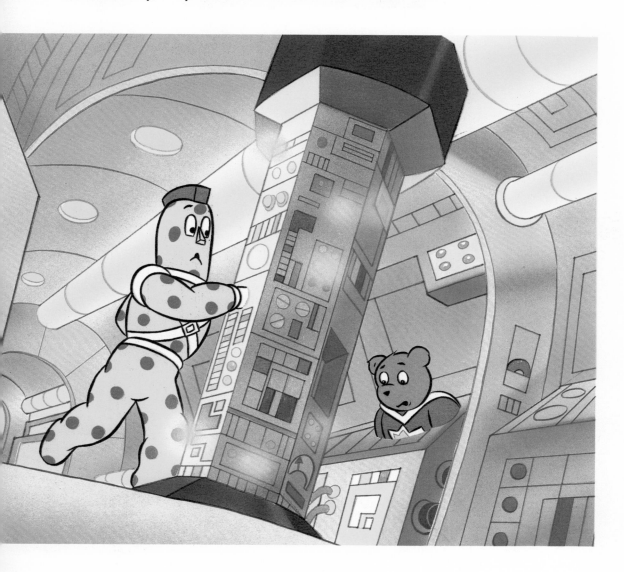

SuperTed and Spotty whirled round in amazement. At the other side of the room was the ghostliest astronaut they had ever seen.

She wore a shiny helmet, and a sparkling suit. Long, luminous hair hung over her glistening shoulders. But the strangest thing of all was that you could see straight through her.

"Rocketing Raspberries!" gasped SuperTed. "It's a ghost!"

"Don't be ridiculous!" said the woman. "There's no such thing. I'm a perfectly ordinary person from the Luminous Planet, where everything is made out of light."

"B..b.." Spotty was so frightened that he could not speak.

"And what I want to know," the shiny stranger continued, "is why you didn't stop after you crashed through my rocket."

"We didn't know it was real," SuperTed explained. "We thought it was a ghost rocket, and we were frightened."

"That's no excuse," said the woman, sternly. "You should have stopped to see if I was all right."

"W..well," burbled Spotty. "Are you all right."

"I'm all right," replied the strange woman, "but you've damaged my rocket."

"How can we help you, then?" said Spotty. "Your rocket's made out of light. We can't even feel it, let alone repair it." With that, he sank through the floor, and dropped into the crater outside.

The luminous stranger called after him. "But you've got a laser haven't you?"

A laser is like a torch with a beam so thin and powerful that it can cut through metal. SuperTed had one in the spotty rocket. He went back to fetch it.

When he returned, the sparkling woman asked him to shine it at her rocket. Slowly, her spaceship began to glow with a brilliant light. Then she seemed to bend the light and smooth it over a dark patch on the side of her rocket.

"That's better," she said, and climbed back into the control room. "Thank you and goodbye," she called "And remember, if you have another accident in space like that, you should stop."

Then there was a flash of light, and the glowing rocket soared away into the sky.

SuperTed and Spotty climbed back into their rocket and set out once more for the Planet Spot

When they got there, Spotty tried to walk through the wall of his dome.

"Ouch!" he cried. Then he laughed. "I got so used to that strange rocket, that I forgot."

SUPERTED

AND THE STOLEN ROCKET SHIP

SuperTed and Spottyman have been invited by a famous scientist to watch the launch of the world's latest rocketship. Three astronauts will travel deeper into space than any man has ever been before.

The scientist points at the astronauts, 'Those brave men will fly to the planets of the Milky Way.'

'Milky Way? I went there for my summer holidays,' exclaimed Spottyman.

'Spotty, Shh . . .,' whispered SuperTed.

'There go the astronauts making their way to the capsule,' said the scientist.

'Mmm, I wonder?' thought a puzzled SuperTed.

Meanwhile, behind the launch pad those villains Bulk, Skeleton and Texas Pete, have captured the astronauts and stolen their spacesuits.

'Ha! Ha! See, I told you becoming an astronaut is as easy as falling off a log,' laughed Texas Pete.

Skeleton is, as usual, worried, 'I think we should go back, I don't think we've had the right training for this kind of thing.'

Tex is annoyed, 'What do you mean, I trained you, didn't I?'

'Yes, but only to rob a bank!' moaned Skeleton.

From the control room everything looks normal. The countdown begins: 10,9,8,7,6,5,4,3,2,1, we have lift off!

As the rocket speeds into the sky, SuperTed looks worried. 'I don't like it Spotty . . . there was something funny about those spacesuits. I know what it was! They didn't fit properly. Quick Spotty, let's go!'

The chums find the astronauts tied up with rattlesnakes and shaking with fear.

As SuperTed untied the snakes, he said, 'You see, if you're kind to them they won't hurt you.'

'Gee thanks . . . saved by a teddy bear,' said the astronaut.

'There's only one person who would tie people up with a rattlesnake . . . Texas Pete. Hm . . . I'll say my magic word.' Whoosh — the teddy bear changes into SuperTed. 'We'll use your rocket, Spotty.'

'Yes,' replied the proud Spottyman. 'It's the only one fast enough to catch them.'

Thousands of miles away, all is quiet in the stolen rocket.
Texas Pete, Bulk and Skeleton are all fast asleep. Tex
begins to dream . . . *'I'm Texas Pete, ruler of the universe.
I'll round up every planet and have it branded with my
name in big letters! I'll be more famous then Billy the Kid!'*
Suddenly he wakes up to find himself in mid air. 'Hey we're
floating!'

Bulk's nose hits a red button. 'Ouch!' he moans and the
rocket speeds off out of control.

Speeding through space in the Spottyship, SuperTed and Spottyman look carefully at the radar screen.

'I can't see anything but spots,' said the confused Teddy.

'Look! There they are,' pointed Spotty. 'It's jumping around like an excited pony.'

'Right Spotty, let's get after them.'

Still floating helplessly inside the spacecraft, the villains struggle to regain control. Tex is clinging to a chair, 'Get off my leg Skeleton. You're pulling down my pants.'

'But I've got nothing else to hold on to.'

Bulk, looking out of the window, upside down, sees the Spotty spaceship.

'Tex, look at that lovely rocket out there.'

Just at that moment they collide with a small meteor. Their spaceship is damaged.

Tex shouts, 'You idiots! Get out there and stick those bits back on.'

Bulk and Skeleton float through the hatch outside the spacecraft.

'This is great,' shouts the stupid Bulk, 'I can fly.'

All of a sudden they hear a whoosh, it's the Spotty spaceship. 'Oh no,' they chorus, 'Not that terrible teddy!'

The Spotty ship collides with Skeleton, puncturing his suit. 'Ooow,' squeals Skeleton, 'I can't move a muscle . . . not surprising, I haven't got any muscles. Boo hoo hoo!' he begins to cry.

SuperTed, his rocket boots on full power, zooms at Bulk. 'Your turn next, Bulk!'

He breaks the air tube to Bulk's spacesuit and blows up the suit like a balloon.

'Don't, you mustn't!' shouts Bulk. SuperTed lets go and the unfortunate Bulk speeds, zig-zagging, through space.

Texas Pete, still in his stolen rocket, starts up the motor to make his escape, and blasts SuperTed with the rocket exhaust and flames. The brave teddy is sent spinning head over heels.

Spottyman races across to him. 'SuperTed, are you all right? Wake up, you'll have to stop him or he'll cause chaos across the cosmos.'

SuperTed is a bit giddy.

'I'm all right, just knocked a bit of the stuffing out of me. Bubbling Blancmange, where's Texas Pete, we must go after him. Come on!'

Meanwhile, Texas Pete has a wicked idea, 'Look, there's that Spotty rocketship, I'll ram it out of existence. Then they'll never get home again.'

Spottyman shouts a warning, 'Look, he's going to ram my lovely rocket. Get him SuperTed!'

SuperTed speeds to the stolen rocket, and clinging on desperately, uses all his strength to bend open the hatch and dive inside.

'Get your nasty paws off me, you horrid little teddy bear!' warns Texas Pete.

'Don't toy around with me, Texas. Take that!' SuperTed hits Texas Pete on the head with his paw, and the silly baddie's head spins round until he thinks he's seeing stars.